Bedtime for Albie

For Bill and Yvette
with love and thanks
for all your support

CANDLEWICK PRESS

First US edition 2021 • Library of Congress Catalog Card Number pending • ISBN 978-1-5362-1118-4 • This book was typeset in Archer. The illustrations were done in watercolor and colored pencil.
Candlewick Press, 99 Dover Street, Somerville, Massachusetts 02144 • www.candlewick.com
Printed in Humen, Dongguan, China • 20 21 22 23 24 25 APS 10 9 8 7 6 5 4 3 2 1

Bedtime for Albie

SOPHIE AMBROSE

There was a rosy-pink glow in the sky
as the sun was sinking down low.
All the animals knew it was time for bed.
Everyone except for . . .

Albie.

"Come on, Albie. It's bedtime now," said Mommy.

"Bedtime?" asked Albie. "Not now!
It's time for rolling and jumping,
sniffling and snuffling. Not bedtime!"
And before Mommy could do anything to stop him,
Albie dashed off!
Skippety trot trit trot.

He went all the way through
the long swishy grass until . . .
"Hi, cheetahs!" said Albie.
"How about a running race?"

"Not now, Albie! We're having our bedtime story.

We'll race you in the morning!"

So off skipped Albie.

Skippety trot trit trot.

He whooshed right into a clear blue pool of water.

"Hi, elephants!" said Albie.

"Want to play splish-and-splash?"

"Not now, Albie! We're having our bedtime shower.

We'll play splish-and-splash in the morning!"

So off ran Albie.

Until he came to the deep-down burrow.

"Hi, meerkats!" said Albie.

"Let's see who can dig the deepest hole!"

"Not now, Albie!
We're very sleepy.
We'll dig holes with you
in the morning!"
So off snuffled Albie.
Skippety trot trit trot.

"I don't want to go to bed yet," said Albie.

"I want to roll and jump and sniffle and snuffle!

If nobody will play with me, I'll just play by myself."

And off he went. *Skippety trot trit trot.*

But it was dusk and the sky was really getting dark now.
Albie could hear mysterious noises all around him.

The rustlings and scratchings of the night.

Hissss!

"Who's there?" asked Albie in a small voice.

"Hi, Albie," said Snake. "It's just me!"

Albie trotted on a little farther.

He saw a pair of big eyes glinting at him in the bushes!

Toowit toowoo! "W-what's that?" stuttered Albie.

"Hi, Albie," said Owl. "It's just me! Shouldn't you be in bed?"

The stars were twinkling in the warm night sky.
"I don't want to play by myself anymore,"
Albie said sleepily. "I just want my mommy."

He snuffled and sniffled—

and came across a familiar,
wet, muddy smell.

Then he snuffled and sniffled
some more until . . .

"Hi, Albie!" said the hippos.

"Let's get you home!"

Mommy and Albie snuggled up tight.

"I'm ready for bed now," said Albie.

"Thank goodness," said Mommy.

"But before you go to bed . . .

it's time for your mud bath!"

Albie rolled and jumped and splished and splashed!

It was the best game he had played all day.

In fact, it was so much fun . . .

that all of Albie's friends wanted to join in, too!
They had the gloopiest, splashiest, noisiest
mud bath party under the stars ever!

Until . . .

it really was bedtime for Albie.

"Night night, Albie."